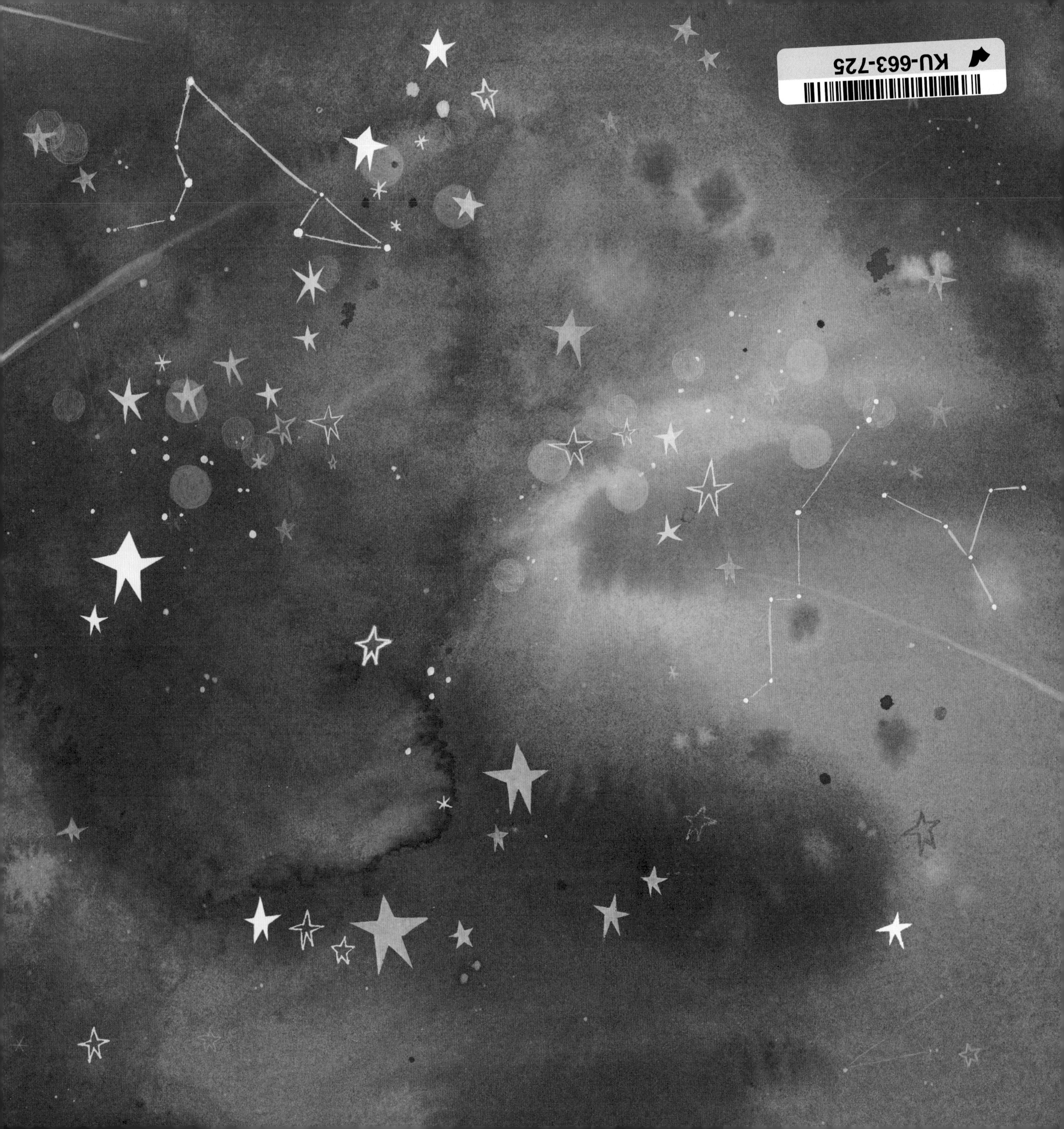

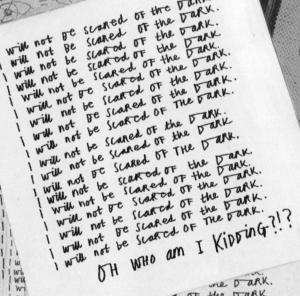

FOR ALEX x

I will not be scared of the dark.
I will not be scared of the dark.
I will not be scared of the dark.
I will not be scared of the dark.
I will not be scared of the dark.
I will not be scared of the dark.
I will not be scared of the dark.
I will not be scared of the dark.
I will not be scared of the dark
I will not be scared of the dark
I will not be scared of the dark.
I will not be scared of THE dark.
I will not be scared of the dark.
I will not be scared of the dark.
I will not be scared of the dark.
I will not be scared of the dark.
I will not be scared of the dark.
I will not be scared of THE dark.

OH WHO am I KIDDING ?!?

I will not be scared of the dark.
I will not be scared of THE dark.
I will not be scared of the dark.

THE BIG Book of OWL'S

A TEMPLAR BOOK

First published in the UK by Templar Publishing,
an imprint of The Templar Company Limited,
Deepdene Lodge, Deepdene Avenue, Dorking,
Surrey, RH5 4AT, UK
www.templarco.co.uk

Copyright © 2014 by Emma Yarlett

10 9 8 7 6 5 4 3 2 1

ISBN 978-1-78370-028-8 Hardback
ISBN 978-1-78370-029-5 Paperback

Edited by LIBBY HAMILTON

Printed in CHINA

HENRY THE GLOW WORM

***ORION
AND THE
DARK

templar publishing

My name is ORION.
and I guess you could say
I am scared of a lot of things.

Mum tells me I just have
a big imagination and there's
nothing to be frightened of...

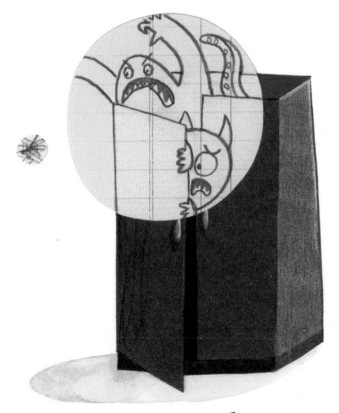

Well, that's easy for **her** to say.

As far as I can see, the world is **full** of frightening things.

But there is one thing that scares me more than anything else…

It's bedtime again.

I hate bedtime.

The night that changed everything, began like any other.
I kept an eye out for monsters…
I kept an ear out for scary noises…

But as it got darker…

and darker…

and darker…

I couldn't take it anymore.

And that's when something strange happened.

Outside my window the Dark seemed to come alive!

And a **thing** I'd never seen before dropped in for a visit.

I was feeling more scared than **ever before**.
(Even more than when I went to that seaside dogshow with Gran.)

But Mum always says it is important to remember your manners,
especially when you are greeting ~~monsters~~ visitors.

So I said,

And offered to shake hands.

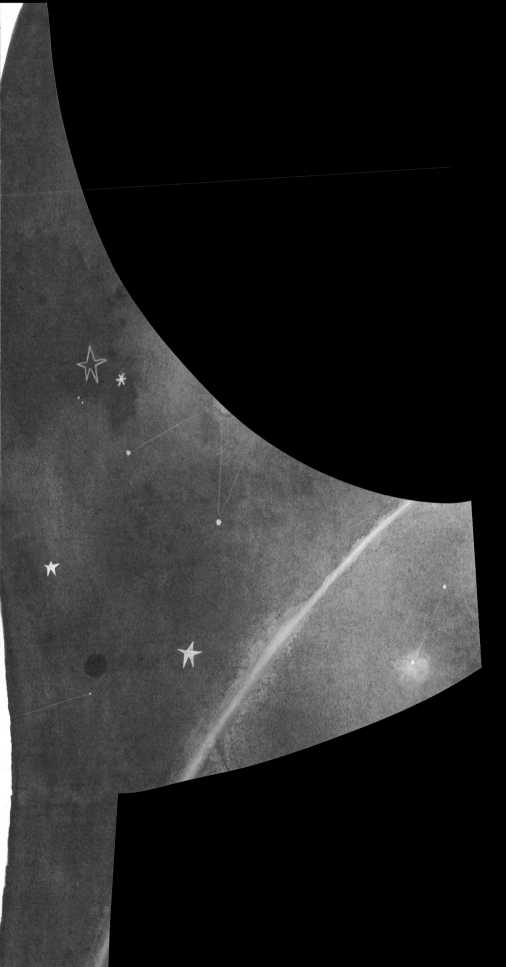

Hello there,
I'm DARK.
Now, Orion...
It's time for you to stop
being so afraid of everything.
Especially me!
Let's go on an
adventure.

Of course, **normally** I'd be scared stiff of going on an adventure, **especially** with a terrifying creature like Dark...

... except this "Dark" wasn't quite what I had expected.

First, he asked to see the **shadowy** and **scary** bits of the house –
the nooks and crannies where the **monsters** live.

1. IN THE WARDROBE

2. Under THE Bed

3. DOWN THE PLUGHole

4. In THE Basement

BOUNCE

The most
FUN!

Look at
my RABBIT
SHADOW!

Even having fun couldn't stop me
from being scared for long though.

Dark asked me if I had stopped feeling afraid.

The horrible wiggly feeling had definitely gone a bit…

But there was still one place that made my knees wobble and my tummy twist with **fright**…

And so off we went…

On one last adventure, all the way up into the **night** sky.

There, in the darkest place of all, suddenly I knew.

When I stopped worrying about being scared…

Dark could be fun,
and Dark could be interesting,
and Dark could be magical.

And most of all…

Dark could be my friend.
And nobody (not even me) is scared of their best friend.

But…

too soon…

we had…

to go…

home.

As the sun began to climb back up into the sky,
my friend began to fade. It was time to say goodbye.

DARK, I've had such a SUPER DUPER, SPIFFADOCIOUS, INCREDAMUNDO ADVENTURE... But will you EVER come BACK?

I didn't want Dark to go.

And from that night on…

he never was.